The Field of the Dogs

Also by Katherine Paterson

Angels & Other Strangers
Bridge to Terabithia
The Great Gilly Hopkins
Jacob Have I Loved
The King's Equal
The Master Puppeteer
Of Nightingales That Weep
Preacher's Boy
The Sign of the Chrysanthemum

I Can Read Books:
Marvin's Best Christmas Present Ever
The Smallest Cow in the World

The *Field* of the *Dogs*

KATHERINE PATERSON

Illustrations by EMILY ARNOLD McCULLY

HarperCollins*Publishers*

For Justin Peter Heininger
the only real Vermonter in the family
with love from us all

The Field of the Dogs
Text copyright © 2001 by Minna Murra, Inc.
Illustrations copyright © 2001 by Emily Arnold McCully
HarperCollins Children's Books, a division of HarperCollins Publishers,
1350 Avenue of the Americas, New York, NY 10019.
www.harperchildrens.com
Library of Congress Cataloging-in-Publication Data
Paterson, Katherine.
The field of the dogs / Katherine Paterson.
p.   cm.
Summary: Josh, who has just moved to Vermont with his mother, stepfather, and new baby
brother, must deal with the bullying of a neighbor boy and discovers that his dog, whom he
hears talking with other dogs, is also facing a bully of his own.
ISBN 0-06-029474-4 — ISBN 0-06-029475-2 (lib. bdg.)
[1. Dogs—Fiction.   2. Bullies—Fiction.   3. Stepfathers—Fiction.]   I. Title.
PZ7.P273 Fi   2001   00-32038
[Fic]—dc21
3   4   5   6   7   8   9   10
❖
First Edition

Contents

CHAPTER ONE

Josh

I wonder where he's going in all this snow, thought Josh as he pressed his nose against a small pane in the porch door and watched his dog bound up the road. Manch would take a great leap and land—and then, instead of sinking into the depths of the snow, the small brown body would bounce up again as graceful as a deer on the nature channel. Where could he be headed? Beyond that stupid Wes Rockett's house, there was nothing at the end of the road—some fields, a bit of woods. Josh had wandered up the road himself last week before the snow came. It seemed strange his mother hadn't stopped him. In Virginia she would hardly let him go to the

1

mall with his buddies. But now with a new husband, a new baby, and an old farmhouse at the other end of nowhere, she didn't seem to care whether he lived or died.

"D'you let Manch out again?" His mother had come to the door with the baby on her left hip and a diaper in her right hand.

"He was asking to go out," Josh said.

"In all this snow? Josh, that fool dog will get lost and freeze to death. I told you to walk him on the leash. He hasn't lived here long enough to find his way home."

Josh sighed, got his jacket, and stuck the leash in the pocket. As he opened the porch door, his mother called from the bathroom. "Have you got your boots on?"

He went back for his boots. The boots were new. Greg, his stepfather, had bought them for him last Saturday—so he could be "a real Vermonter." What a laugh. He yanked off his old sneakers and then pulled on the boots, huge rubber bottoms and leather tops that had to be laced up practically to his belly button. At this rate the dog would be miles away before Josh even got off the porch.

"Don't stay out too long, now," his mother called again. "If you can't find him right away, just come on home, hear?"

"Yeah." Josh slammed the door and started down the porch steps, which wore six to eight inches of snow. Before dawn someone had plowed the dirt road that ran in front of the house, but there were already another four or five inches of snow on it. As he picked up one heavily booted foot and then the other, Josh remembered how Manch had bounded across the snow like a deer.

He passed the Rocketts' house as quickly as he could. No sign of Wes. That bully. At the bus stop on Josh's first day of school, Wes had grabbed him and stuffed snow down his jacket. So Josh started a new school cold and wet and furious. Wes was still laughing about his "snow job."

Well, one good thing about snow. He could follow Manch's happy tracks with very little difficulty. Tracking. Josh's imagination shifted into gear. In his head he pictured the chief ranger speaking to him, Josh Wilkinson. *"There's a rabid wolf out there somewhere, Wilkinson. We're counting on you to track it down."*

I should have brought the gun, thought Josh. *I know how to handle it. A guy shouldn't just walk out alone into the wilds of Vermont unprotected.* But the gun was locked in the gun cabinet, the shells someplace else entirely. "It's not a matter of trusting or not trusting," his stepfather had said. "Just sensible safety precautions."

Josh grabbed a dead branch. Carefully, he raised it to his shoulder and sighted along the slightly curved length. *When I see him,* Josh thought, *I get him right between the eyes, no second chances in a situation like this.* He was out of sight of the Rocketts' house now. The road dead-ended into another. The tracks of the "rabid wolf" had now become only part of a pattern of tracks. *A pack of wolves?* Josh said to himself. *How many are rabid?* His blood froze. Would he have to shoot more than one? Would he have time? Courageously he pushed

4

forward, following the tangled pattern of prints off the road through a small woods. He entered the line of trees cautiously. He might be a courageous forest ranger, but he was no man's fool.

Suddenly a sound broke into his daydream. What was it? Dogs, he thought. But how could dogs make that sound? It was like laughter—wild, not quite human laughter.

CHAPTER TWO

The Field of the Dogs

Josh shook his head, as if to make sure he had completely thrown off his daydream. But, no, it was laughter, he was sure, though not any laughter he had ever heard before.

The woods ended abruptly in an expanse of dazzling whiteness. He squinted against the sun. There, in the dip of the hill, he saw them. Three—no, four—dogs in the middle of the snow-covered field. One, a large tannish mongrel, was lying in the snow. The other three were leaping across its body, landing on the other side, and rolling and tumbling against one another in the snow. All of them were laughing.

Finally, the big dog staggered to his feet and

shook himself. The little cocker spaniel, who had landed on the big one's back just as he stood, went flying several feet across the snow. Manch and the smaller black-and-white mutt threw their bodies into the large dog with a tackle that sent them all sprawling. It was their laughter that Josh had heard. The dogs were laughing. A chill pierced Josh's chest like an icepick.

The dogs were playing like children. For a few minutes Josh stood silent, watching. The longer he watched, the more he wanted to run out and throw his own body into the heap, but something held him back. Perhaps he shouldn't be here. Perhaps he had stumbled onto something that was none of his business. It was as though Manch had another existence in which he wasn't a pet dog, but someone with his own life and special friends to share it with. Just as Josh himself would have if his dad hadn't died—if his mother hadn't met Greg on that stupid ski trip—if he was still in Virginia with his friends . . .

A cloud covered the sun. More snow was on

the way. Josh had better get home. He turned his back on the field and started through the woods. Then he heard them. The dogs were coming too, still panting from their game. Josh dodged behind a tree.

"We've got to make some rules for you, Ace." The voice, full of importance, seemed to belong to Manch, though how Josh knew this was a mystery. "It takes two of us to get you down, sometimes all three."

Ace seemed to consider this. "Well, it's always three to one. Twelve legs to four."

"But the length of the legs, shouldn't that be considered?" The tiny black-and-white dog who looked to be part terrier was craning his neck to look up into the face of the huge dog.

"And Honey's a girl." Manch indicated the spaniel.

"It's size, not gender, that matters," she said with a sigh.

"Well, if all of you think I'm so much better . . ."

"Bigger, not better," said Honey a bit huffily.

10

She turned toward the little terrier. "Right, Wicker?"

"Oh, Honey, what does it matter?" said the terrier. "We're all avoiding the issue. What are we going to do about the River Gang, Manch? They said yesterday the field was their territory and if we dared come here again . . . They're all as big as Ace. What are we going to do if . . ."

"Fight," said Ace. "I've been playing in this field since I was a pup. No flatlander mutt is going to scare me away."

"Ace!" protested Honey, nodding her head toward Manch.

Manch laughed his eerie dog laugh. "Oh, that doesn't hurt my feelings, Honey. I'm from the flatlands and I'm a mutt. No getting around it."

"It's not the same," said Wicker. "You came here as a friend and you've already stood up against those bullies with a bite out of the big guy's ear to prove it."

"Hush up!" Manch, who was in the lead, stopped suddenly, his nose quivering. The others froze.

"What is it?" asked Ace in what he must have thought was a dog whisper. "The River Gang?"

"Shhh, no," Manch warned. "Worse."

CHAPTER THREE

Worse Than the River Gang

"What could be worse than the River Gang?"
Honey whispered anxiously. "What is it?"

"People odor," said Wicker softly.

The dogs waited on the edge of the woods
as Manch strolled in carelessly, took a deep
sniff, and ran straight for Josh's tree. He
jumped up on the boy, wagging his tail and
yapping.

It was signal to the others, who im-
mediately began wagging their tails and
barking.

Later, Josh wondered why he had messed
up everything. If only he'd pretended not to
have seen or heard them earlier. Why hadn't
he just taken out the leash, snapped it on,

and ordered Manch to come home? Perhaps he spoke as he did because he was lonely. He had made no friends in the two weeks he'd been in the new school. Perhaps the longing to belong to someone—to be a part of a gang of kids as he had been in Virginia—was too much. At any rate, he did speak and nothing was the same afterward.

"You bunch of fakes," he said. Josh had meant to sound like he was teasing, but it came out wrong. "I saw you. I heard you laughing and talking." The dogs, if they understood, made a good show of pretending they hadn't, wagging their tails and panting.

"Just who in the heck is this River Gang you're so scared of?" Josh asked.

Still no sign from the dogs. "I could help you, you know. Find out stuff. Spy. Dogs wouldn't suspect a human." He hated the way his voice was going up, as though he was desperate. "Don't give me this dumb act, guys. I *saw* you. I *heard* you. I'm on to you."

But the dogs didn't stay to listen. Manch jerked his head and raced out of the woods, the other three dogs in pursuit, leaving Josh alone, jiggling that stupid leash.

"Sorry, son, snow days are over. They've got all the back roads plowed and the school buses are running again." Greg was standing over Josh's bed, a mug of steaming coffee in his hand. Josh burrowed deeper under the covers. He wished his stepfather wouldn't call him "son."

"I've got the woodstove burning in the kitchen. You might want to dress in there. It's cold as a dog's nose in here."

Dogs. Had he really seen them? Heard them? Or was it his stupid imagination?

"It's after seven. The bus won't wait."

Good, thought Josh, and turned his back on Greg. *I can stay home and follow the dogs again. They'll have to . . .* have to what? They didn't have to do anything. They were dogs. *I'll tell on them,* Josh thought. *Tell who? Greg? He'd just laugh. Mom? She'd take me to a psychiatrist. The kids at school? Yeah, sure. They think I'm weird enough already.*

15

"Josh!" His mother had replaced his stepfather beside his bed. "If you think I'm going to put up with your—"

"I'm UP!" he yelled, throwing the covers back so violently that his mother stepped back from the bed to get out of his way. "Honestly."

"Honestly, what?" his mother asked. Her eyes were flashing. Just then the baby started to cry, and without a word she turned and left the room. *Yeah, whatever the little fellow needs. Run to him.* The room was freezing cold. Greg and his woodstove! Josh pulled on his clothes as fast as he could, but his fingers were shaking so, he could hardly manage the buttons. *It's child abuse, that's what it is. It's too cold for human beings in this house, in this whole state.*

He went over to the window and peered out. It wasn't even dawn yet. He might as well live at the North Pole, where the sun never rose all winter long. *Sheesh.*

Suddenly, he heard a sound—dogs barking,

lots of dogs. Then he saw them, black forms against the white of the snow—Manch and his gang with a pack of huge dogs right on their heels.

CHAPTER FOUR

Problems

Josh had to get outside fast and help Manch. He began to dress more quickly.

"Josh!" His mother was yelling up from the kitchen. "Stop your dallying and come down here this minute!"

The dogs were in trouble! What could he do? He should have talked them into letting him join them yesterday. After all, he was human. He had access—well, he would have access—to a gun. Greg's gun. With a gun he could at least scare off the River Gang. Wes Rockett had a gun. He was always bragging about it.

"Joshua Anthony Wilkinson!"

"I'm coming!" He clattered down the stairs.

His mother was spooning cereal into the baby, but she looked up when he came in. "Well," she said, "that's better. Your oatmeal's getting colder by the minute."

"I don't have time to eat," Josh said, hurrying toward the door. Greg lowered his newspaper. "Can't wait to get back to school, hey?" He winked, another of his "let's be pals" tricks, and went back behind the paper.

Before Josh got across the room, there was a familiar scratch at the porch door. "Josh, will you let the dog in?" his mother asked. But Josh was already opening the door.

"Are you okay?" he whispered.

Manch ignored him, walking in, head high, tail awag. He went, as he always did, to his food dish, sniffed, then went to the water dish and, finding it empty, stepped on the edge of the bowl and set it clanking.

Just ask for it, boy. Go ahead, I dare you. What would his parents do if Manch opened his muzzle and said a few words? Ha! *No, don't do that, boy. I want to be the only one who knows.*

Manch clanked the bowl again.

"Okay, okay, boy, I get the message," Greg said, starting to fold the paper.

"I'll get it!" Josh said. He jumped for the bowl, filled it at the sink, and then put it on the floor again, near the woodstove. Greg was watching him. "Smart dog, that one." It was what he always said when Manch rattled the water dish. "He can always tell you what he wants."

If you only knew. Josh stood watching as Manch lapped away, sloshing the water on the floor like he was some ordinary dog.

"Josh, you've got to sit down and eat your breakfast."

Josh obeyed, his eyes on the dog. Now Manch had gone and got his rubber bone. He brought it to Greg and stood up on his hind legs to drop the toy into Greg's lap. "Hey, hey, this isn't playtime, you old lug. I got to go to work." Manch ran to the center of the big kitchen and sat, his head cocked to one side. "Okay, okay, we'll show them our trick. Loves to show off, this character. Jeanie, Josh, watch this." Greg threw the rubber bone. The dog jumped, snatching it midair. "See that? Right out of the air? Smart boy!"

Josh watched, a giggle growing in his throat. *Smart boy, indeed.*

Manch carried the bone back to Greg and dropped it in his lap. Greg put his face down into the dog's. "Woof!" the man said. Manch cocked his head in mock surprise and then, tail wagging like a propeller, splashed his tongue all over Greg's face.

If you only knew, Josh said to himself, *if you could only hear him talk.* The giggle Josh had been holding back burst out in a great snort. Everyone looked at him, even the baby.

"Hey, what's so funny?" Greg asked in a pleased, puzzled kind of way.

"Nothing. Just something I happened to think of," said Josh.

"By the way," said Greg. "I ran into Fred Rockett at the post office yesterday." Josh's

blood froze at the name "Rockett." Greg went on. "He says his kid brother can't wait to get to know you better. He's in your class, right?"

Suddenly Josh wasn't hungry. *Wants to get to know me better—nothing,* he said to himself. *Wes Rockett wants to kill me.*

CHAPTER FIVE

The Bully

"Thought you might be sick, little flatlander," Wes sneered as Josh came toward the bus stop. Wes loomed head and shoulders taller than the kids around him.

"Yeah," one of the little guys said. "Thought it might be too cold for you."

Luckily the bus came. Josh jumped on and headed for the only open seat, which was right behind Mrs. Lynch, the driver. Wes walked past him to the rear. Josh relaxed, then tensed up. Wes was coming back up the aisle. "Sit down, Wes," the bus driver yelled.

"Okay, Mrs. Lynch," Wes said, sliding in beside Josh.

Josh shoved himself up against the window.

25

"Hey, Flathead." Wes smiled, sticking his big nose right into Josh's face. "Forgot to tell you. We have kind of an initiation for flatlanders. You know Carter's Woods?"

Josh shook his head.

"Sure you do. Just down the road from your house"—he smiled—"and mine. We'll expect you there after school today." He tweaked Josh's nose, making Josh pull back even farther. "Guys who don't show up for the ceremonies are always sorry. Get it?"

Josh nodded again. He felt like such a wimp.

He could hardly get through the day. Every time his mind would wander for a moment, there would be Wes in his face, smiling or mumbling something like "See ya, Flathead. Don't forget."

How could he forget? His stomach turned whenever he thought about it. Then he remembered the dogs. He'd get them to help. The bullies would be afraid to attack him with Manch and Ace snarling beside him. But how could he persuade Manch? If anything, the dog was mad at him for yesterday. *But he's my dog. Dog is man's best friend, right? Oh, right.*

Manch was gone when Josh got home. "Where's Manch?" he asked his mother.

"Oh, probably out playing with his pals," his mother said.

"What?" *How could she know?* "What pals?"

His mother was feeding the baby and reading a book at the same time and certainly not paying much attention to him.

"What do you mean, pals?"

"I'm joking, Josh. I don't know where he is. He wanted to go out and you weren't home yet and the baby had to be fed—"

"You shouldn't do that! Just let him out. You said yourself he doesn't know his way around here."

She looked up at him. *Good*, thought Josh. *She feels guilty.* "I'm sorry, Josh, I just had too much—"

"Never mind. I'll go look for him." *And hope*

to heaven, Josh said to himself, *I find him before Wes and his gang find me.*

"Take the leash!" she called after him, but he pretended he hadn't heard her.

The snow on the road had been packed down since yesterday, so he ran—ran as fast as his clumsy boots would allow. He had to find the dogs before Wes found him. He tried to figure out a way to cut down to the field and avoid Rockett's house and the woods altogether, but the snow was so high that he was afraid it would slow him down too much to leave the road.

There was no sign of Wes and company as he passed the Rocketts'. He raced into the woods, around the trees, tripping over trunks and bushes half hidden by the snow. His cheeks were hot and he was panting like a mutt when he came to the edge and saw the dogs playing down in the field. He stumbled down the hill toward them, falling on his face just short of them. Manch came running over, wagging his stupid tail, nosing Josh's neck.

"You got to help me, Manch. Don't act like you don't understand. A bunch of guys are coming to beat me up! Listen! That's them now! You gotta help! Please! They'll kill me!"

CHAPTER SIX

The Confrontation

Lying there on his stomach in the snow, Josh was sure he could hear Wes Rockett's gang coming through the woods laughing and talking, but Manch gave no sign that he had heard. The dog just wagged his tail and then leaned down and licked Josh's chapped cheek. "Cut it out! Don't act stupid. I need you." Josh struggled to his feet. Manch jumped up on Josh's legs, wagging and woofing. "Quit it. I mean it!"

"There he is!"

Josh turned. Five boys stood at the top of hill. "You coming up, Flathead? Or do we have to come down and get you?"

He looked at the dogs. They gave no sign

that they would help him. Even Manch, *his own dog*, was hanging back as though there was no connection between them. As though he didn't even know Josh. *I've owned you since I was six,* he wanted to say, but he didn't. In fact, the mutt had never looked doggier and dumber in his life. So much for man's best friend. There was no escape.

Josh started up the hill. He felt like he was going to his own execution. He could hear the boys at the top of the hill whispering and giggling. What were they planning to do? Beat him up? Tie him to a tree? What did Vermont bullies consider "initiation" for a flatlander? It was so unfair. He hadn't wanted to come to this stupid state in the first place.

He walked slowly, his eyes on his boots. For once he didn't curse their heaviness. If he kicked, kicked with all his might, maybe he could get out of this with nothing broken. He counted the dark figures at the top of the hill furtively. There were five of them. If he kicked the little guy on Wes Rockett's right—

"What's taking you so long, flatlander?

Lead in your pants?"

All the boys laughed.

"C'mon, guys. Let's meet the poor little punk halfway." Wes started down the slope, the other four right behind.

"Manch, please, you got to help me." Josh turned his head and begged in a desperate whisper.

But Manch only wagged his tail. Ace, Wicker, and Honey did the same. Whatever Manch did, they would follow his lead. And none of them were about to help Josh.

"If you scare these guys off, I'll help you with the River Gang. Really. I could be a big help."

"Who you talking to, flatlander? Your little imaginary friend?"

"I was talking to my dog," Josh muttered.

"Nice dog," Wes said, sounding almost sincere. "I'm a sucker for dogs. Too bad this poor fellow has to live with *you*."

"What are you going to do?"

"Do you hear that, guys? He wants the details of the initiation. We don't give out that kind of information in advance, do we, guys?"

"Naw," they chorused.

"It's a surprise, Flathead. Anyone got a scarf?"

The small kid snatched one from around his neck. "You can use mine, Wes," he said, all eager-eyed to please.

"Okay. Now who wants to practice their knots? Jackson—you're a Boy Scout. Tie his hands behind him in a regulation Boy Scout knot."

Jackson grinned. "Sure thing, Wes." He grabbed the scarf.

Should I kick the Boy Scout? Josh wondered. But it was too late. Jackson was behind him. He'd have no strength kicking backward. He wanted to yell out at Manch—*"Sick 'em!"* or *"Kill!"* or something—but how could you tell a dog whose tongue is lolling out and whose tail is wagging to charge? What was the matter with the stupid dog? Didn't he care what happened to Josh?

Jackson tied the scarf tight around Josh's wrists. *I'm such a wimp. Why didn't I at least try to get away?* But how could he? There were five

of them—all used to moving in snow.

Suddenly the little guy gasped and pointed up the hill. At the top stood a huge silver-gray dog with ice-blue eyes, his lip curled, his teeth bared in a snarl.

CHAPTER SEVEN

Run!

The snarling silver-gray dog was flanked by four dogs almost his size. All of them with bared teeth. Josh shivered. This must be the River Gang.

After that first gasp the boys were still as rocks. Fear had caught in their throats as they stared in horror at the line of dogs watching them, teeth sharp and gleaming white in the failing light. Time was as frozen and silent as the winter field.

Josh, his wrists still bound by the scarf, stood as still as the rest. No one seemed to know what might happen if anyone, boy or dog, moved. Finally he was aware of a nose nudging the back of his knee. He looked back to see Manch pushing at him. *He wants me to run for it,* Josh decided. No one was looking at Josh anymore. Now was the time.

He was afraid they would hear him and turn on him, his boots crunched so loudly in the snow, his panicked breath coming in great steam-engine pants. But no one, boy or dog, seemed to notice. He wriggled his hands out of the scarf—Boy Scout knot, indeed—and dropped it behind him as he went. When he was well into the woods, he heard a terrible snarl, a scream, and then the sounds of all hell breaking loose.

He didn't go back; he couldn't. He ran.

The quick, early dark of December was already closing in by the time he got to the house. He fumbled at the doorknob, and when the door opened, he almost fell into the house.

"What's the matter?" His mother had come running from the kitchen to the mudroom. She was worried about him. The first time she'd acted worried about him since the baby was born last summer.

"Nothing," he said. He mustn't cry. Mustn't

let on. He pushed past her into the kitchen.

"Where's Manch?"

"I dunno."

"Are you all right, Josh?"

"Yes. I told you already!"

"Take off your boots before—"

"Awright. Awright. I'm taking off the stupid boots!" What had he done? He'd run, that's what. Turned tail and run. He tried to tell himself that Manch had made him run—but it was no comfort. He had run. No one would ever forget that.

Josh sat down heavily on a kitchen stool and ripped at his bootlaces. Angrily he yanked at the toe of one boot and then the other; next, tears threatening to blind him again, he unlaced the hated things from top to halfway down. He clawed at the right boot until he could pull it off his foot.

"Josh?" Now she was hovering over him. When he least wanted her to notice him, she was all concerned and so close he could smell the baby odor that always clung to her nowadays. He flung off the second boot.

"Leave me alone!" he cried, and raced sock-footed to his bedroom.

He stared out the window into the dark. *Where is that blasted dog?* He had to know what had happened since he left the woods. From down the hall he could hear the sounds of the washing machine filling. He glanced at his watch. As dark as it was, it wasn't even half past four. She wouldn't start fixing supper yet. If only the baby would start yelling. Then he could sneak out again. Where was that kid when Josh needed him? He was aware suddenly that his socks were wet and his feet on the bare wood felt like ice. He got himself some dry socks and sat down on the bed to rub his feet back to life. *Where is Manch?* he asked himself again. *Why hasn't he come home?*

Good. The baby was sounding off. Josh waited until his mother came up the stairs past his room, and then he tiptoed down to the kitchen and, taking his boots to the mudroom, slipped them on. He grabbed his jacket and flew out the door.

It was freezing in the darkness, and he'd forgotten to bring a flashlight. He started to turn back when he heard, far off in the distance, a wail—the sound of an animal in terrible pain.

CHAPTER EIGHT

Ace in a Hole

Once more he heard the wail. Should he go back into the house and get a flashlight? He'd have to. He couldn't even see to tie his boots out here past the porch light. He opened the door softly. His mother was still upstairs. He could hear her talking to the baby as he laced the boots. Then he crept in and grabbed the flashlight from the top of the refrigerator.

"Greg?" his mother's voice called from upstairs.

"No, it's only me," he answered.

Just then behind him, there was a loud thump, like something hurled against the door. He hurried through the mudroom to open it. It was Manch, his eyes wild with fear.

43

He opened the door wider, but the dog didn't come in. He was quivering, his tail down.

"It's Ace," the dog muttered. "You got to come."

They had left the porch and were well down the road before Josh realized what had happened. Manch had dropped the act. The dog had actually spoken to him. He hadn't just imagined it.

He didn't try to talk to Manch as they walked, just switched on the big flashlight and followed behind as fast as he could. *Durnit,* he thought. If only he'd remembered his gloves. His hand was freezing on the metal shaft of the flashlight. He switched to his left hand and buried his right in his pocket. His ears and face were aching from the cold. He yanked up the hood of his jacket, but it fell back down. This was crazy. Even if they found Ace, what was Josh supposed to do? He'd never be able to carry the big dog. And suppose he was lying dead someplace? Then what?

"I'm going back," he said. "It's too cold. I'll

freeze to death before we find him."

Manch turned and looked at him.

"Well, say something. If he's hurt, I can't carry him."

Manch cocked his head, but he didn't speak. Maybe Josh had only imagined the other times. Mom always said he had too big an imagination.

"Please, Manch, I'm dying out here."

At this the dog ran ahead, beyond the beam of the flashlight. Josh ran after him, and then the bobbing light caught something large and yellow against the white of the road.

"Ace!"

He ran over to the big dog. Manch stood over his head, licking his friend's face, as though trying to lick him into consciousness.

Josh knelt down in the icy snow of the dirt road. Was Ace breathing?

Yes, he was breathing, but not easily. He was badly hurt. "Did that big silver dog get him?"

"At first. But Ace would have won except for the plow," Manch said dully. "He was fighting the weimaraner and not watching."

45

There was no doubt. Manch had spoken that time, but Josh knew he shouldn't call attention to the fact. "I'll get Greg," he said. "We need the pickup to get him to a vet."

Manch didn't follow. He seemed to be standing guard.

"Where have you been? You had me worried sick, Josh."

Josh brushed off his mother's hand. "Greg. Where's Greg?"

"He's not home yet. It's barely five." His mother smiled. She was pleased he wanted Greg for whatever reason.

"Then call him. Now."

"What in the world's wrong? Josh? What's the matter?"

"Mom! Call him, will you? Oh, what's his number? I'll call him myself."

Greg came at once, but still it was after six before they got back to where Manch stood guard over his big friend. "A snowplow hit him," Josh said, and then realized he shouldn't know what had happened. "Or something like that. I think he's hurt bad."

Greg knelt over the big dog as though to listen for his breathing, then he felt the fur around his great neck.

"He's alive, isn't he?" Josh asked anxiously. "He's not dead?"

CHAPTER NINE

Plotting Revenge

Greg shook his head. "It doesn't look too good. Get the blankets from behind the seat, and then we'll lift him up. Good boy," he murmured to Ace, stooping down to stroke his back.

Manch was jumping about nervously, watching their every move. "Go home, boy."

"Can't Manch ride up front with me?"

"Oh, all right. But he'll have to stay in the cab. We can't be bothered with him at the vet's. He'll just get in the way."

"You want me to help you carry him in?" Josh asked fearfully, as they pulled up at the vet's.

"No," said Greg. "I can manage."

Josh and Manch watched Greg carry Ace from the back of the truck into the clinic. Josh had told Greg he'd wait in the cab with the dog. Greg shook his head. "Well, if you get too cold . . . it's subzero out here—"

Josh tried to talk to Manch, but the dog had gone mutt dumb on him. "Yeah, when you needed me you could talk all right." But Manch just curled into a ball on the seat and closed his eyes. Like a stupid dog who didn't know squat.

Josh's teeth began to chatter. "Well, if you won't talk, I'm going in. I'm not freezing my tail for nothing." He climbed out of the truck and slammed the heavy door as hard as he could. "Catch me helping you again," he muttered.

Just then Josh spotted Greg coming out of the clinic door. He looked grim as death. "Will he? Is he?"

"He's dying," Greg said. "Dr. Walters is trying to locate his owner. He'll have to be put down."

"Put down?" Josh's lips felt frozen.

"Get in the truck, son. There's nothing we can do here."

They rode for several miles in silence. Josh could feel Manch's body quivering against his thigh. *Put down? No!*

"They can't just kill him," he said finally.

"I'm sorry, Josh, but he's not young. He's had a good life."

"But you can't just . . . like . . . he's—he's a friend of Manch's."

Greg gave a short laugh.

"No, really. Dogs have friends."

Greg patted his knee. "Sure, kid."

Josh lay awake for hours trying to figure out what to do. He was in on their secret now, and they needed him. Surely they'd realize that without Ace they would be helpless against the River Gang—dogs twice their size and trained to be mean. He remembered that silver-gray coat and those icy eyes and shivered under his quilt.

Poor Ace. And it's all my fault. Manch made those dogs fight so I could get away safe. Somehow

I'll make it up to them. Somehow.

When Wes Rockett got on the school bus the next morning, he headed straight for Josh's seat. "Where did you go in such a hurry yesterday?"

Josh looked out the window, pretending he hadn't heard.

"You there, Flathead." Wes thumped Josh on the head. "I'm talking to you."

"I—I went to try to get help." Nobody needed to tell him how lame he sounded.

Wes snorted. "Yeah. I just bet. Good thing for you your dogs aren't as chicken as you are."

"My dogs?"

"Yeah. The big yellow mutt and the weimaraner took a few bites out of each other. Then the whole pack went yapping away." He laughed his snorting laugh. "You missed all the fun."

Josh gave Wes a quick look. Had he been scared? Of course he had. All of them had been scared witless by that weird-a-whatever.

"We still haven't had your initiation, you know," Wes said.

"Yeah?" Josh tried to sound tough.

"Me and the guys decided. No big deal. We just want you to get the weimaraner's collar for us. *Bring it to me by tomorrow.*"

CHAPTER TEN

The Gun

Josh sat through his classes, hardly knowing what was going on. Ace was probably dead by now, killed by that stupid vet. Manch was likely to blame him for that—hadn't he taken Ace to the vet's? And now Josh had to figure out a way to get the weirdhammer's collar or be branded a coward for life.

To Josh's surprise, when he got home Manch was curled up on his cushion by the wood-stove. His eyes were closed, but something told Josh that the dog was no more asleep than he was. How come he wasn't out there with Wicker and Honey, plotting revenge? Didn't he care about Ace at all? Josh asked himself. Or was the dog as big a sissy as his master?

Master—ha! Well, he *was* the master. Whatever the last two days had meant, that hadn't
changed. He owned the stupid dog. It was up
to him, Josh, to fix things.

"Don't you want your snack?"

"Huh?" Josh must have been a million miles
away. It took him a few seconds to focus on
the milk and the peanut butter sandwich his
mother had put down on the kitchen counter
under his nose. "Oh, yeah, thanks." He took a
bite and tried to smile. With one of Greg's
guns he could just kill the weirdhammer—
that would break up the River Gang *and*,
when the silver dog was dead, taking the collar
would be no sweat. The thought of killing a
dog, any dog, bothered him, but this was a
vicious dog. Nobody should own a dog that
was a threat to other dogs—even to people. Or
if you did own one, you shouldn't let it run
loose. No, killing this particular dog would be
like police work—sort of.

He'd have to plan it out carefully. He
couldn't afford to mess up. Stealing the bullets
out of Greg's bureau would be easy. The gun in

plain sight in the glass-fronted cabinet would prove harder, but if he was just patient, he could find the key.

After supper that evening, while Greg and his mother were watching TV in the living room, Josh crept upstairs in his sock feet. The bullets were easy to find. Greg had several boxes of shells stacked in the side of his bottom bureau drawer, but the key was not with them. Josh could hear the TV. Once Greg laughed out loud and then said something to Josh's mother. He couldn't make out the words. *Where's the blinking key?* he asked himself.

The baby lay sleeping in the corner of the room. Josh glanced his way, but he seemed peaceful, making funny little noises as he breathed. Josh tried to stuff a box of shells into his jeans pocket, but it was too big. He stuck it under his sweatshirt and held on with his left hand while he scoured the room for the key. Where would Greg keep it?

He pulled open all the bureau drawers as quietly as he could, looking each time at the baby to make sure he didn't wake up. Suppose they came up to check on the kid? What excuse could Josh give them for being in their room, rifling through their drawers? He began to sweat. *Cool it!* he commanded himself. *They're in the middle of a show. Just think.* Where might Greg keep the key? He wasn't a secretive guy. It was probably in a totally obvious place—like the box there, on top of the bureau.

The box was wooden with a carved top. Josh lifted the lid. At first he didn't see what he was looking for, covered as it was with cuff links, screws, buttons, and coins, but there it was, a shiny silvery metal key. It must be the one. Josh fished it out and stuck it in his pocket, swirling the other junk around a bit to cover the spot. The gun would be harder to steal, but after school when his mother was busy with the baby he'd have a chance.

Manch, still on his cushion the next afternoon, opened his eyes when Josh crept into the kitchen with the key. "Yeah, I'm getting the gun," Josh muttered. "You're doing

nothing. Well, someone around here cares about Ace." The key turned easily in the lock and the cabinet opened with a bare click of the handle. Still, Josh stopped, listening for any sound of his mother's footsteps. *Which of the four rifles could it be?* he wondered.

"Joshua? What are you doing out there?"

"Nothing!" His voice broke. She knew he was up to something. She was sure to come in and catch him messing with the guns.

CHAPTER ELEVEN

Facing the Enemy

"Josh? Do I need to come in and check on you like you're a four year old?"

"No ma'am." He was sweating like fury. He waited, his heart pounding until he heard her say:

"You behave yourself, now."

"Yes ma'am." He began to work faster. He reached under his shirt for the shell box. *How could you tell which shells fit which gun?* Josh wondered. He lifted the lightest-looking rifle out of the case. He didn't dare try loading the bullets in the kitchen. His mother was likely to pop in anytime. Heart beating so loud that he was afraid she'd hear from her bedroom, he closed the cabinet door, locked it, and carried the gun and shells up to his own room and shut the door.

With a bit of fumbling he managed to break open the rifle. The shells were too large. Back to the kitchen for another try. It took three to make the match. But by then his mother had come down the stairs and was bustling about the kitchen, throwing the eternal laundry into the washer, singing, and talking to the baby.

Josh took out the shell (he wasn't an idiot) and stuck the unloaded rifle down his pant leg. If his mom was as absentminded as she usually was, she wouldn't notice, would hardly question his going out. "C'mon boy," he said to Manch as he passed through the kitchen. The rifle made him drag his left leg, but maybe she wouldn't turn around.

He got himself to the mudroom and then yelled back. "Just going out—be back in a minute."

"Take the dog, won't you? He's hardly been out all day."

"Here, Manch, here, boy!" Josh gave a whistle, but the dog still didn't budge from the cushion. Josh couldn't wait. He hurried as fast as he could, the rifle keeping his leg stiff like a sort of splint. After he got down the porch steps, he went around the edge of the house, pulled out the gun, and began to run down the road as fast as he could.

If Manch wouldn't help him, surely Wicker and Honey would. They had to help him find the River Gang before dark. The gun had to be back in place before Greg got home from work. His mother would never notice a missing rifle, but he knew his stepfather would.

Josh saw the two little dogs before they saw him. From the edge of the woods he watched for a minute. They looked lost against the snow of the field. From time to time they glanced up toward the woods as though they were waiting for something—for someone.

When the dogs saw Josh emerge from the woods, they didn't start toward him. They just stood there, staring dully.

"Ace is dead," he said, when he got to where they stood waiting. "Or will be. He was hurt so bad, the vet is going to put him to sleep."

Both dogs' heads jerked at the news, but then they went into their sniffing doggie act. He ignored it.

"I brought this gun, see? And I'm going to get that silver dog. You got to help me find him."

But the little dogs weren't listening. They were looking beyond him to the woods. Josh turned around. The silver dog was there, just like the last time, flanked by the four other huge dogs that made up the River Gang. Josh fumbled with the box, dropped it into the snow, then put down the gun to get out the shells. His hands were freezing and shaking.

At last he got out a couple of shells, broke the gun over his knee, and inserted them. His forehead dripped with sweat. It seemed to take hours. He could hear the low growls of the River Gang from the top of the hill, but he didn't dare look up. He had to be ready to shoot before he looked at them again.

Where was the stupid safety? He was all thumbs—and every thumb a block of ice.

Cripes! They'd kill him before he even got the gun ready to shoot. There! He swung the gun up and took aim through the sights.

"*RRRRRRRRaw!*"

CHAPTER TWELVE

Disaster

With a snarl the River Gang charged down the hill. Josh pulled the trigger, but the shot went wild and the kick against his shoulder knocked him backward. Still off balance, he shot again, but this shot went somewhere over the heads of the coming dogs. The sound of gunfire froze the dogs in their tracks. But then Josh fell, dropping the gun, and they came angrily to life.

Josh screamed, and just as he did so, a brown figure raced down the hill and threw itself into the gang, scattering them across the snow. Josh struggled to his feet and began to run as fast as he could through the drifts. He could hear the growls and snarls and yaps of pain behind him

but he didn't stop. He had to get away.

But where could he go? If Greg didn't kill him for stealing the gun, his mother surely would. He stopped running. *I'm not going to spend my life running,* he thought. *It's time to use my head and not my feet. If I run now, Manch will die. And it will be all my fault.* But Josh knew he couldn't stop the fight alone. He needed help, and there was only one person close enough. He tried to figure out what to say as he ran. He couldn't give the dogs away. He had already caused them too much harm.

Tears started in his eyes. He wiped them away with his sleeve. He couldn't cry. This was no time for acting the baby. He was staggering with exhaustion by the time he got to the door. He banged on it.

"What the—?"

"Rockett. You got to come. I need your help."

Wes cocked his head. "You're asking *me* for help, Flathead?"

"Please. I got no one else."

He stared at Josh. "You got nerve asking me to help you."

"I know. I know. But you got to come anyway. The big yellow dog—the one that chased off the silver one—"

"Weimaraner." Wes obviously liked saying the word.

"He got hit by a snowplow . . ."

"Yeah, I heard."

He wanted to ask Wes how he knew, but then around here people seemed to know everything—everything about their neighbors and their neighbors' animals. *Except one thing. They don't know that dogs can talk,* Josh said to himself. He went on aloud. "Well, I was trying to figure out how to keep that weird—that dog from getting anybody else killed and I was trying to get the stupid collar—like you said— but my shot missed—"

"You were going to *shoot* the dog? You idiot! You weren't supposed to shoot the dog!"

"I—I didn't know how else to get the stupid collar. Anyhow I messed up and I think he's going to kill my dog."

Wes cocked his head. "Yeah?"

Josh could hear the desperation in his own voice. He was sure Wes could too. "He—Manch—my dog doesn't have any sense. He'll fight someone three times his size."

"Kind of like his owner, huh?"

"I didn't fight you."

"You probably would have—sometime."

"What makes you think I would?"

"Anybody crazy enough to go after that weimaraner's collar is crazy enough to go after me." He sighed, then gave a half grin. "Wait up. I'll get my things."

They ran down the road to the woods, Wes trying to zip his jacket as he ran. "Don't shoot dogs, Flathead," he said.

"But you said I had to get the collar—"

"I never thought you'd *try*, you idiot." Wes stopped suddenly, grabbing his arm. "What's that noise?"

It was the noise of snarls and yaps and growls, but almost in slow motion, as if the

71

dogs had fought to the point of exhaustion. The boys crept to the edge of the trees and peered down. Below was a tangle of furry coats.

"Look!" whispered Wes. "Blood!"

CHAPTER THIRTEEN

Rockett to the Rescue

Wes was pointing down the bank. "Look," he said, "down there on the snow. That's blood for sure."

Josh peered down to where Wes was pointing. There was no mistaking it—the dark, almost-black red against the white of the snow. He swallowed hard. Manch's blood, more than likely. He was the one who had hurled himself into the pack. *And he did it to save my hide,* Josh knew.

Now it was up to Josh to save Manch. But what could he do? A dog like that wirer—whatever—could kill a kid his size. *Think. Think.* Of course. The solution was staring him in the face.

Snow. The perfect weapon. He scooped up a handful, but he couldn't press it into a ball.

Wes laughed quietly. "Where did you live before, flatlander? Virginia? This snow is too dry. You can't make balls with it."

From below came what sounded almost like a human cry. Someone was really hurt.

"Bark!" he yelped to Wes. "Howl! Anything! We got to distract them."

Wes let out a long, wolflike howl. Once again the dogs froze in place, lifting their noses in the air.

Josh flung himself down the hill and into the pack, yanking up Manch. "It's a wolf!" he yelled. "Run for your lives!"

The River Gang took off like a shot. Whether or not they understood him, he'd never know. But between them, he and Wes had somehow frightened the stupid creatures away.

Manch was wriggling in his grasp. He put the dog down on the snow. Blood was smeared all over his fur. "Can you walk?" Josh asked. The dog shook himself and started up the hill, limping, but struggling through the deep snow on his own.

"I got to get the gun," Josh muttered and went back to get it. The shells were scattered about. He couldn't take the time to get them.

Wes met him at the top of the hill, grinning. "Hey! You were great. But I wasn't bad, either, was I? Pretty good wolf, huh?"

"Yeah, thanks." They walked along together, following Manch. The farther they went, the worse his limp seemed. *Oh, God, please,* Josh prayed, *don't let him be really hurt.*

"Where'd you get the gun?"

Josh looked down at his hand. "I—I took it from my stepfather. He'll probably kill me."

Wes laughed. "My dad would," he said and then, watching Manch's painful progress through the snow, "I'll get my brother to drive us to the vet's."

Wes's brother elected to wait in the pickup. "Can't stand the sight of blood," he muttered.

Josh looked down. He hadn't realized how much blood was smeared across the front of his jacket. "You don't need to wait," he said to the Rocketts. "I'll call Greg to come get me—us."

"You go on, Fred," Wes said. "Tell Mom I'll be late."

Josh wanted to thank Wes, but he was afraid he might choke up. This was the guy that he'd hated so. "You don't have to," he said finally.

Wes grabbed the gun off the backseat, daring his brother to say something. Fred opened his mouth, then just shook his head.

Wes slammed the cab door shut. "See ya later," he yelled at his brother, and then to Josh: "I just gotta see if the little mutt's okay." He grinned. "I'm a fool for dogs."

Wes held the heavy door of the vet's office open as Josh carried Manch in. A blast of hot air from the woodstove greeted them, making Josh realize that he had been shivering. The waiting room was empty. Josh wondered momentarily where the receptionist had got to—but maybe in Vermont, vets didn't have receptionists. He sat down, holding Manch carefully on his lap.

Suddenly he was aware of voices—somebody yelling curses from a back room. "What's going on?" he asked Wes in a whisper.

"Shh!" answered Wes. "Sounds like a fight!"

CHAPTER FOURTEEN

Friends and Fears

"Okay," the voice from the back room yelled, "Okay! So he can just come home to die, then. I'm not putting him down. Suppose somebody'd took a notion to put me down that time I lost three fingers in a mower? Jeezums Crow, Doc. This dog is at least as tough as me!" The yelling voice cracked then, as though the speaker might burst into tears any moment.

There was a soothing reply in a woman's voice, the words of which were too soft to make out. Josh and Wes looked at each other. Wes nodded. "It's old Jake Tidwell fighting for Ace."

"Who's the woman?"

"The vet, dummy. Dr. Walters."

Before too long a tall leathery-skinned man emerged from the back carrying a huge yellow dog in his arms, followed by a tired-looking young woman in a none-too-clean white coat. Wes jumped to his feet. Josh started up, but a whimper from Manch stopped him. Ace raised his head a painful inch off his master's arm and gave a weak wag of his tail.

The old man's face softened. "These fellers friends?"

"Yeah," said Josh. "Friends. I hope he makes it."

"Yours, too," Jake Tidwell said as Wes opened the door for the old man to go out.

"Help him get Ace into his truck, will you, Wes?" the vet called out. "Looks like I got my hands full in here." She shook her head. "What's going on here? Has every dog in the county gone crazy? I just treated a weimaraner a couple of days ago."

Josh carried Manch into the back and laid him gently down on the metal table. The vet let out a low sigh as she examined him.

"Doesn't this little guy know to pick on someone his own size?"

"He's going to be all right, isn't he?" Josh asked.

The vet sighed. "I hope so. Punctures, you see. Pretty deep. Your biggest worry here is infection. If you can keep 'em clean, they ought to heal up all right. Can you do that?"

Josh nodded. He could do anything. He had to.

"Bring him back next week. Or earlier if he doesn't seem to be getting better."

"Okay. And ma'am," he hardly dared ask. "Will Ace make it?"

"I wouldn't have given him a nickel's chance yesterday. Today—who knows?"

Josh called his mom and asked her to send Greg to pick them up. She got all worried on the phone, but he would only tell her that Manch had been in a fight and they were at the vet's. No, no, Josh wasn't hurt. He didn't mention the gun. He couldn't. How was he going to sneak it back into the house?

"They'll kill me," he said to Wes as they

waited for Greg to come, "when they find out I took the gun."

"Act sincere," Wes advised. "It's the old George Washington and the cherry tree routine. Parents are suckers for sincere."

But Josh was not convinced.

Greg didn't glance at Wes or the gun as he entered the waiting room. He came at once to Manch and inspected all his wounds. "How could this happen?" he asked Josh. "The poor thing."

"He was trying to protect me," Josh said. "It was those dogs that came the day of the—you know—the day you . . ."

"Flatlanders," Wes said contemptuously, forgetting for the moment that that was one of his favorite names for Josh. "Soon as they move to Vermont they buy these huge dogs—without a flea's notion how to train 'em. They're letting these idiot dogs just run wild . . ."

The vet nodded. "This is the third dog I've treated this week. Of course Ace was hit, but still, something funny is going on around here . . ."

"Well, I guess we'd better get this poor

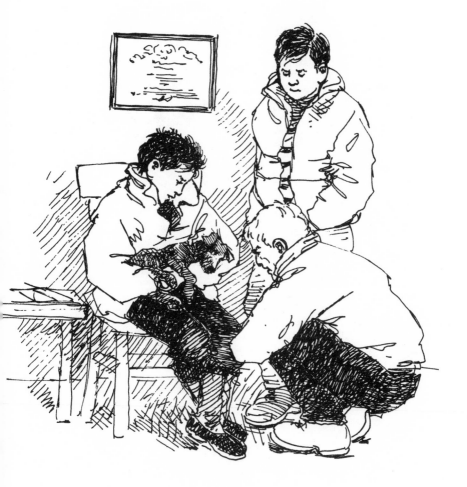

old fellow home," Greg said. "You all right carrying him, Josh?"

"Yessir." He got up carefully. Wes followed, trying to keep the gun out of Greg's sight as he walked. But when they got to the door, Greg stopped to hold it for the boys.

"What the hey? Where did that gun come from?" *This is it.* He was going to get it now. Greg would kill him.

CHAPTER FIFTEEN

Beyond the Field of the Dogs

"It's your gun," Josh said.

"Well, could I ask what it's doing at the vet's? The last time I saw it, it was locked in a case in the kitchen."

"Yessir, it was."

Greg started to say something but seemed to think better of it. He was silent all the way to Wes's. But after seeing Wes safely down his own driveway, he said, "Wes's a good kid. Like some old-time Vermonters, he pretends to be hard on newcomers—"

"Yeah, I know. He's okay."

There was another long pause. "Haven't you been reading the newspapers lately? You could have *killed* somebody with that gun!"

85

Tears started in Josh's eyes. He wiped them away angrily, but this time he couldn't stop them.

"What do I have to do? I thought I'd made sure—"

"You did. It was me. I—I stole the key. But I swear it won't happen again. I *swear*."

Greg studied him closely. "I think you've learned a lesson. I just thank God it wasn't a harder one than this," he said, running a hand across Manch's back. "There'll be locks on the triggers from now on. I can't take any more chances."

"No sir."

"I'm not your dad, Josh. If I were, I'd feel obliged to—"

"To punish me?"

"Yeah." Greg looked at him, not realizing that the pain and disappointment in his eyes were almost more punishment than Josh could take. "I don't beat on kids. It never made much sense to me to hurt a kid to teach him to stop hurting others."

Somehow at the moment Josh would have

preferred a whipping, but he thought of something that might make sense to them both.

"I could baby-sit," he said. "Give Mom some time off."

Greg looked dubious. "I wasn't sure you even liked your brother."

"It'll give me a chance to make friends."

Greg threw him a quick glance. "I'll need to talk to your mother. See what she thinks."

"Yes sir." He couldn't quite say the word "Dad," but maybe, someday . . .

Later that night, Manch picked himself up painfully and headed for the door. Josh jumped up and went out on the porch with him. "I'm sorry I acted so stupid. I'm not interfering again." He started to pick the dog up, but Manch shook his hand off and made his way slowly and painfully down the front steps.

"Look," Josh said when they were out in the far side of the yard with only the moon for light. "Look. This may sound crazy, but Wes Rockett and I are going to be friends. At least,

I *think* we're going to be friends. Who knows, maybe you and that dumb weirdhammer—"

"Weimaraner," said Manch crossly. "And his name is Ghost."

Josh went to the field of the dogs one more time. It was the day after the fight. He felt he had to tell Wicker and Honey that Manch was okay and that Ace—even Ace—might pull through. They stared at him as he spoke, but they never gave even a little yap to let him know they understood. He knew then that the adventure in the field was over—that he'd never belong in the field of the dogs. He sighed as he made his way back up the hill.

The weather was great. He'd stop by the Rocketts'. Before the snow Greg had given him an awesome saucer. Maybe Wes would like to go sliding—

A few weeks later the heavens opened and twelve new inches were dumped down on top of the old snow. Manch scratched at the door to be let out. Before Josh opened it, he leaned over and whispered, "Say hi to Ace for me."

His mother buckled the baby in the high chair and came over to where he stood. She reached over and pulled Josh close.

Josh looked up at her, but she wasn't looking at him. She was staring out a little pane in the door. "Well, thank goodness. He looks good as new, doesn't he?"

For a moment the two of them stood there together, watching the dog bounding down the road like a deer on the nature channel.

"I wonder where he's going in all this snow," she said.

Josh gave her a little hug back. "Who knows?" he said, his eyes following Manch until, at last, the graceful form bounded down the snowy road past the Rocketts' farm and out of sight.